Archer the Therapy Dog
A read together book

written by Katie Baron and
illustrated by Emily Beach

THE BRIGHT & BEAUTIFUL
THERAPY DOGS, INC.

golden-dogs.org

The Bright & Beautiful Therapy Dogs, Inc. is a non-profit 501 (c) (3) all volunteer organization. We do not accept monetary compensation for our visitation.

Katie and Archer are happy to donate a portion of the profits from this book to The Bright and Beautiful Therapy Dogs, Inc.

Illustrations by Emily Beach

ISBN 978-1-989506-92-9

Printed in the United States

For permissions requests, please contact:
Pandamonium Publishing House
pandapublishing8@gmail.com
www.pandamoniumpublishing.com

Disclaimer: The information provided in this book is for educational and informational purposes only. It is not intended as a substitute for professional advice, diagnosis, or treatment. Always seek the advice of your veterinarian, healthcare provider, or therapist with any questions you may have regarding therapy dogs or related matters.

Second Edition 2023

Dedicated to my children, who taught me to be brave, and to my husband, who stuck by me through it all.
- Katie Baron, 2023

Dedicated to my whole family, who I am so grateful for, and to my friends, and to Archer for getting me through the <u>RUFF</u> times.
- Emily Beach, 2023

I dedicate this book to all my brother and sister therapy dogs. Keep making people happy - Woof!
- Archer, 2023

Special thanks to Sara McHugh, Margot Bennett, and Jen Moscone for your time and effort reading, re-reading, and re-reading this book. You are truly appreciated!

Author's Note

I can tell Archer loves when children read to him by his wagging tail and the way his eyes sparkle with happiness. He enjoys hearing the children's voices, getting belly rubs, and having his ears scratched.

Reading to a therapy dog is a great opportunity for children to build confidence by reading to a soft, fuzzy listener who will not judge them if they stumble over a word.

Reading to young children is another wonderful way to foster a love of books and reading.

This book is a Read Together Book. As such, alternating pages are geared towards children and adults, which provides flexibility in the reading experience.

If you or your child (depending on age) read just the pages on the left, you'll enjoy a fun story about how Archer becomes a Therapy Dog and where he goes to visit.

The pages on the right have facts and information related to therapy dogs. You have the option of sharing the facts pages with your child, reading them to yourself, or paraphrasing them based on the age of your child.

This book is designed to educate children and adults, using carefully chosen, age-appropriate language. When children search for hidden Archers, they are developing pattern recognition, which is so important when they begin to learn mathematics. Even the font has been chosen because it's easier for people with dyslexia to decipher. As a person who has dyslexia, loves to read, and was a math major in college, these details are very personal to me. After the 1st edition was published, it was pointed out that the outlined words on some of the children's pages made it difficult for people with ADHD to read. This has been corrected in the 2 nd edition.

Our wish is that this shared reading experience is a powerful tool to unlock the magic of reading for your child.

- Katie & Archer

Notes from Archer's Students

"Archer is a caring, adorable, and loveable Golden Retriever who loves belly rubs, swimming, playing keep away, and cuddling to help calm you down and focus. However, if you don't like dog kisses, don't get too emotionally attached because Archer loves to give kisses while you pet him!" - Charlize F.

"Archer is a very friendly and kind dog, from my experiences with him. Archer is a therapy dog; a therapy dog is a dog that tends to go to libraries and schools. Therapy dogs are supposed to make people calm and happy. Archer is a Golden Retriever that is very playful."
- Kylen C.

"Archer makes me feel more calm when he comes into my class. I have known him for a while, and he is the calmest dog I've met. I love him as a therapy dog!"
- Maddi S.

"Archer makes our day every Tuesday when he comes into school. We are all happy to see him. Archer also helps right before tests and gets rid of stress. Best Golden Retriever EVER!"
- Michael B.

Archer is a Therapy Dog, not an Emotional Support Dog or a Service Dog.

He has been specially raised to be gentle, friendly, and well-behaved. Archer started training when he was 13 weeks old by attending a puppy kindergarten class. As he advanced through the levels of obedience classes, Katie and Archer learned to communicate with each other. It took 2 years of training classes and lots of practice before they were ready to pass the test to become a registered Therapy Dog Team.

As a therapy dog, Archer brings comfort, smiles, and floof to lots of people in lots of places; he is not dedicated to supporting one person like an emotional support dog.

Archer does not get to go on airplanes or into restaurants like a service dog because he doesn't help someone perform a task or help them with a medical condition.

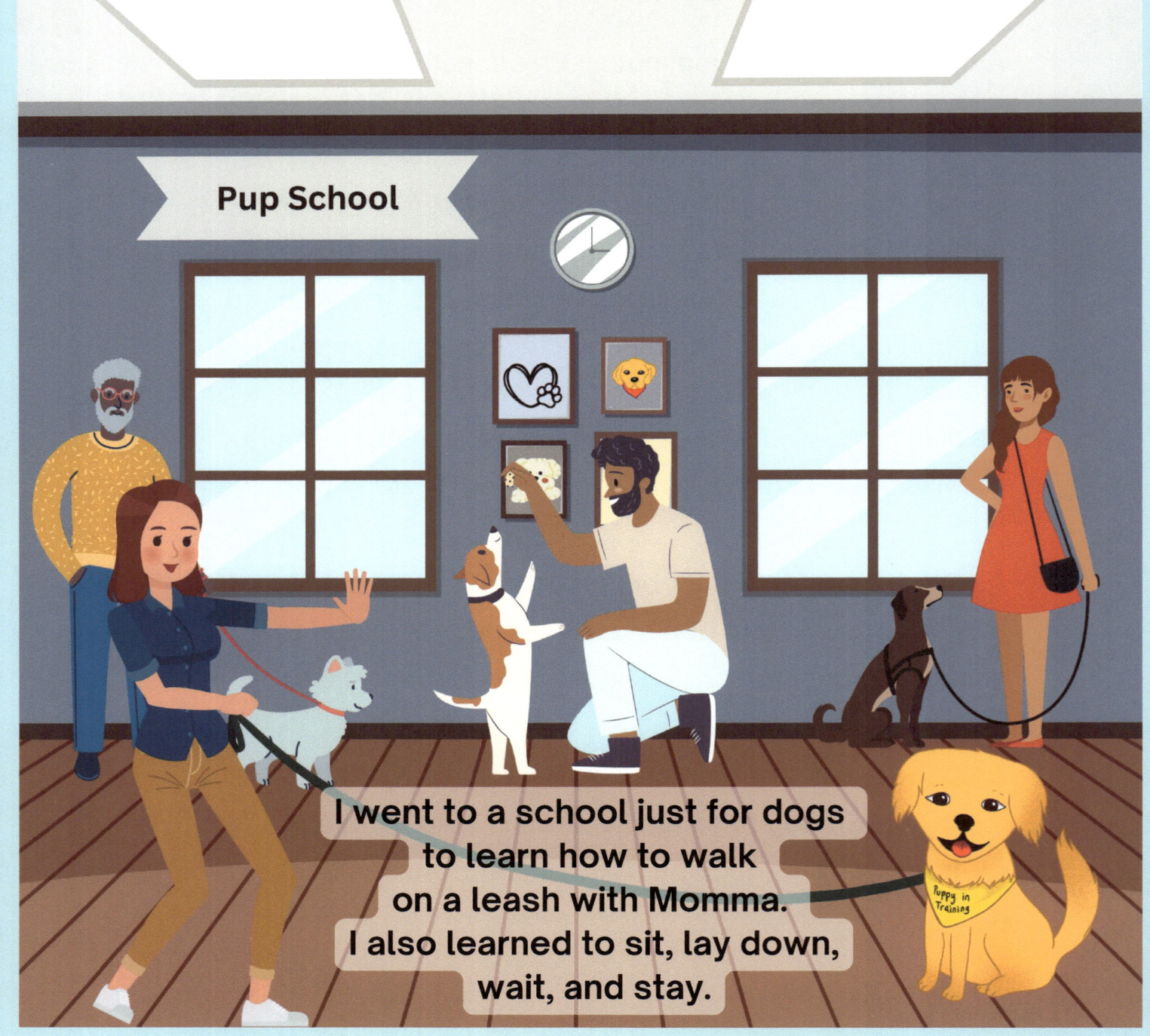

I went to a school just for dogs
to learn how to walk
on a leash with Momma.
I also learned to sit, lay down,
wait, and stay.

Basic obedience is the foundation of therapy dog training. However, not all therapy dog organizations require that a dog go to obedience school to become a therapy dog.

The American Kennel Club (AKC) recognizes over 200 therapy dog organizations on their website, and there are many others as well.

If you are interested in your dog becoming a therapy dog, check with the facility you want to visit to see which therapy dog organization they prefer.

Once you have decided on a therapy dog organization, reach out to them to find out about their guidelines and requirements.

When I was a small, fluffy puppy, I was proud to wear my yellow bandana, so everyone knew I was learning.

Sometimes it's easy to tell if a dog is working because they are wearing a special vest or harness. However, according to the Americans with Disabilities Act (ADA), service dogs, also known as assistance dogs, are not required to wear a patch, tag, vest, or harness identifying them as a service dog.

Therapy dogs, on the other hand, are required to wear identification when working, such as a vest, bandana, id tag, and/or a leash imprinted with the therapy dog organization name. The handler must wear their therapy dog organization id/membership card. Some organizations also require the handler to wear a branded shirt or uniform.

Never approach a dog that is clearly working or assisting its owner because they could be distracted, and the owner may be harmed.

If a dog is wearing a vest, harness, or bandana, take a moment to read it to see if approaching the dog is allowed before asking to pet it.

I am not allowed in the food store, so I stay outside.

Grocery Store

I see lots of people walking in and out, banging carts, and doors that seem to open by magic!

The Americans with Disability Act (ADA) grants public access rights to Service Dogs – dogs that perform a task for a disabled person or that alert their person about a medical condition. Service dogs are allowed everywhere people are allowed.

Under the ADA, Emotional Support Dogs (ESDs) are not considered Service Dogs and therefore do not have public access rights. However, according to the Fair Housing Act (FHA), housing providers cannot refuse to make reasonable accommodations for the owners of assistance animals – which includes service dogs and ESDs.

Therapy dogs are not emotional support dogs or service dogs. Just like any family pet, therapy dogs are not protected by the ADA or the FHA and do not have public access rights.

This means that therapy dogs can only go into pet-friendly stores or hotels and are not permitted in restaurants or on airplanes.*

*Air travel is not covered by the ADA; however, the Air Carrier Access Act (ACAA) definition of a Service Dog is the same as the ADA. The ACAA only grants access to air travel to Service Dogs.

At the park I want to play with the kids, but I learn to sit quietly while the kids run and play with a ball.

Momma gives me a treat and says, "Good boy, Archer."

Training a therapy dog includes teaching them to remain calm and obey commands even when there are lots of distractions, including children and other dogs.

When a therapy dog is working, it should not interact with other animals, including other therapy dogs.

Most therapy dog organizations accept any dog breed as a therapy dog, if the dog has the proper temperament and training. The temperament of the individual dog is more important than the breed. I know some wonderful therapy dogs that are German Shepherds, Doberman Pinschers, or Pit Bulls.

Even the best trained dog may not be a suitable therapy dog. A therapy dog must be friendly and patient with all types of people, including children, the elderly, and people with disabilities. They must be confident and can't be fearful of strangers, new situations, loud noises, or being touched all over.

Now I am calm and gentle when I lay down. People feel better when they rub my belly and pet my soft fur.

Therapy Dogs, Emotional Support Dogs –
What's the difference?

Therapy Dogs are pets that have passed a test to be registered with a therapy dog organization. They have had extra training to remain calm when meeting new people in new situations. Therapy dog teams volunteer to visit schools, hospitals, nursing homes, libraries, court houses, and other places where many people benefit from the support and comfort of petting a dog.

Emotional Support Dogs are also pets, but they provide comfort and support only to their owner and do not have to pass a test or be registered. Their owner must be diagnosed with a mental illness that benefits from an emotional support dog. Emotional Support Dogs are only allowed in restaurants, stores, or airplanes that are pet friendly. However, they are allowed to live in places and stay in hotels that do not allow pets.

Hospitals and nursing homes often have elevators, so it's important for a therapy dog to feel comfortable riding in one.

From a dog's point of view, an elevator is a very small room that can be crowded, and the floor feels like it drops out from under them, which can be unsettling.

Dogs who are fearful or become aggressive in small spaces or crowds may not be suited to be therapy dogs.

Escalators, or even stairs - especially the ones with open risers - can be scary for a dog that has never gone up and down them. Exposing a dog in-training to escalators and different types of stairs will contribute to their success as a therapy dog.

Tip: Escalators are dangerous for dogs with long hair, so avoid them if possible. If an escalator cannot be avoided, hold the dog's tail up so it does not get caught.

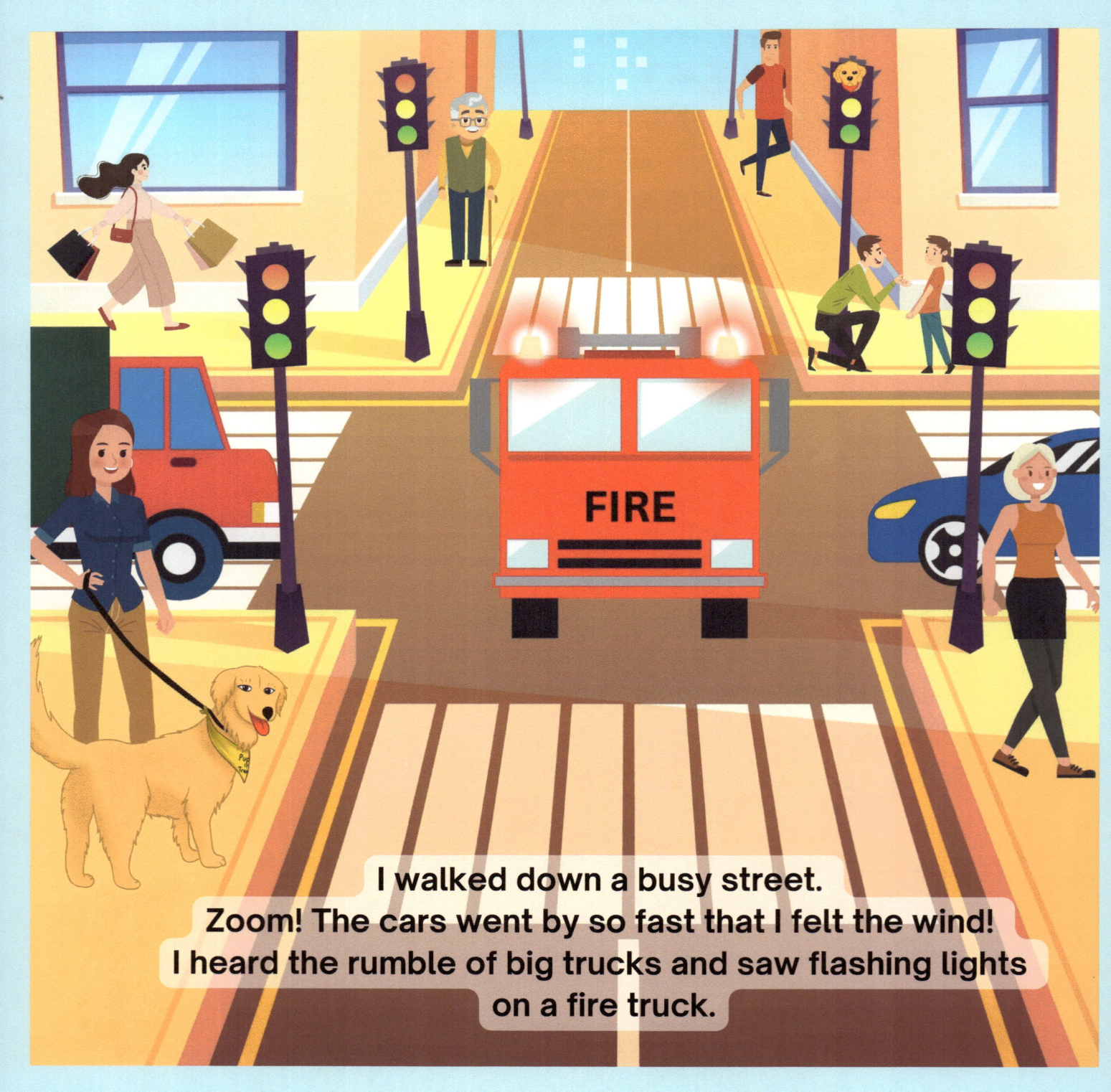

I walked down a busy street.
Zoom! The cars went by so fast that I felt the wind!
I heard the rumble of big trucks and saw flashing lights
on a fire truck.

It is very important to introduce a therapy dog-in-training to lots of places where they can experience different sounds and smells, meet new people, and even walk on different surfaces.

Teaching a puppy or dog to remain calm and focused, without fear or aggression, is called "socialization."

When socializing a dog or puppy, gradually increase the number of distractions. Always reward good behavior with yummy treats and lots of praise. If your dog is fearful, don't push them towards what they fear. Rather, stay on the periphery and give treats and praise. When they relax, take a step closer. Be patient; it can take weeks or months of positive reinforcement to overcome fearful behavior.

"Leave It" is one of the most important commands that a therapy dog learns. It can apply to treats, food dropped on the floor, a person walking by, another dog, and anything that the dog should ignore.

Besides showing admirable restraint and good manners, "Leave It" protects your dog from things that should not be eaten, such as medication dropped on the floor or foods that are bad for dogs.

Foods that are bad for dogs include chocolate, onions, garlic, raisins, grapes, macadamia nuts, avocados, all forms of alcohol, and the artificial sweetener Xylitol. Xylitol can be an ingredient in peanut butter, so if your dog loves peanut butter, check the label.

The therapy dog test is not just about making sure the dog obeys commands; the evaluators are also looking for temperament, general behavior, communication between the handler and the dog, and the handler's control.

It is essential for a therapy dog and its handler to work well together. If a dog has already passed the test with one handler and a second person wants to make visits with the same dog, the dog must re-take the test with the second person.

The dog and handler must be able to manage unexpected situations, such as a crowded room, loud noises, or people behaving erratically.

It is also important that the therapy dog handler understands the rules and guidelines of the therapy dog organization.

Service Dogs and Emotional Support Dogs work with one person – their owner. They have a deep bond and relationship with their person.

Therapy Dogs, on the other hand, are constantly meeting new people in unfamiliar situations. They need to be tested and registered with a therapy dog organization because facilities that invite them to visit need the assurance that the therapy dog can handle new people and situations.

Registered Therapy Dog teams are covered by the organization's insurance, which is necessary when making visits to public facilities.

Archer and Katie are registered with Bright and Beautiful Therapy Dogs, Inc.

Some days I am a Library Dog.

When I go to the library, the kids like to pet my soft fur when they read to me.

Libby likes to peek at me to make sure I am listening.

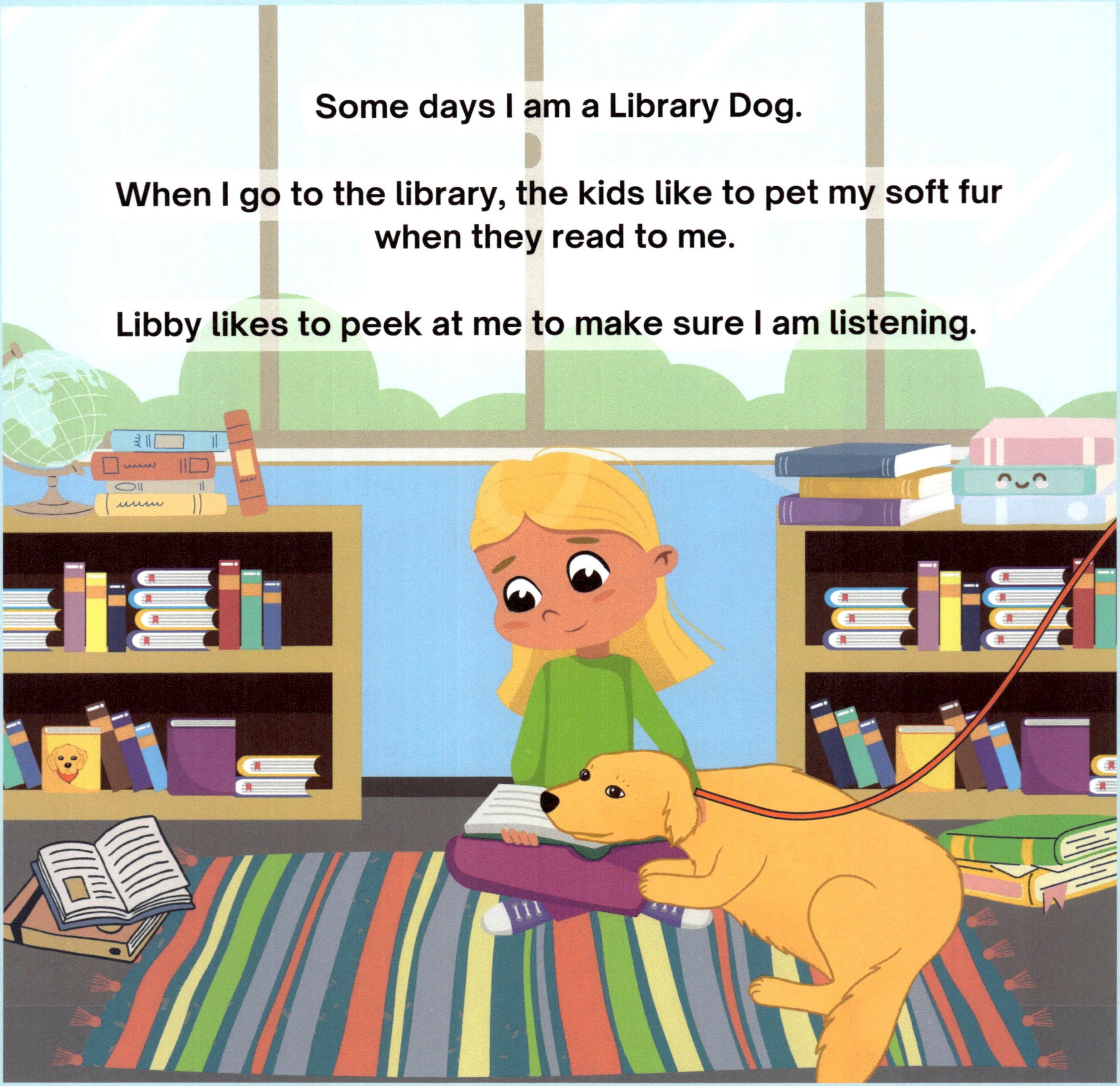

Reading to a dog builds confidence and can improve literacy skills by providing a less stressful environment and a non-judgmental listener.

A University of California, Davis study involving canine reading programs found that students who read to dogs increased their reading fluency by 12% to 30%. 75% of the parents reported that their children read aloud more frequently and with greater confidence after the study was completed. (1)

Reading aloud to a dog also increases a child's communication skills by improving vocal projection and enunciation. A child who masters these skills at a young age may have better public speaking skills later in life.

Some days I am a School Dog.
In one of the rooms I visit, there is a boy named Tommy who is afraid of dogs.

I try not to wiggle too much so I do not scare him.
Every time I see Tommy, he comes a little closer.
Maybe the next time I see him, he will pet me.

The presence of a therapy dog in the classroom can promote a positive and welcoming learning environment.

A therapy dog provides nonjudgmental support, which can help a child feel less stressed and anxious if they are overwhelmed by exams, peer pressure, or even family situations.

Therapy dogs can also help students learn and improve social skills. Children who interact with therapy dogs develop stronger relationships with teachers and peers due to the experience of trust and unconditional support with therapy dogs. A therapy dog can help a child learn to regulate their emotions and express themselves.

If you are meeting a new dog or are scared of a dog, do not try to pet the top of the head because the dog will naturally reach up to try to sniff your hand. It is better to pet under the chin or toward the neck of the dog – away from the teeth.

Some days I am a Hospital dog.

Jack, a very sick man, has been in the hospital for a long time. As Jack talks to me, I listen and wag my tail.

Jack says, "You are so sweet, and your ears are so soft."

I can tell he feels better, so I wag my tail some more.

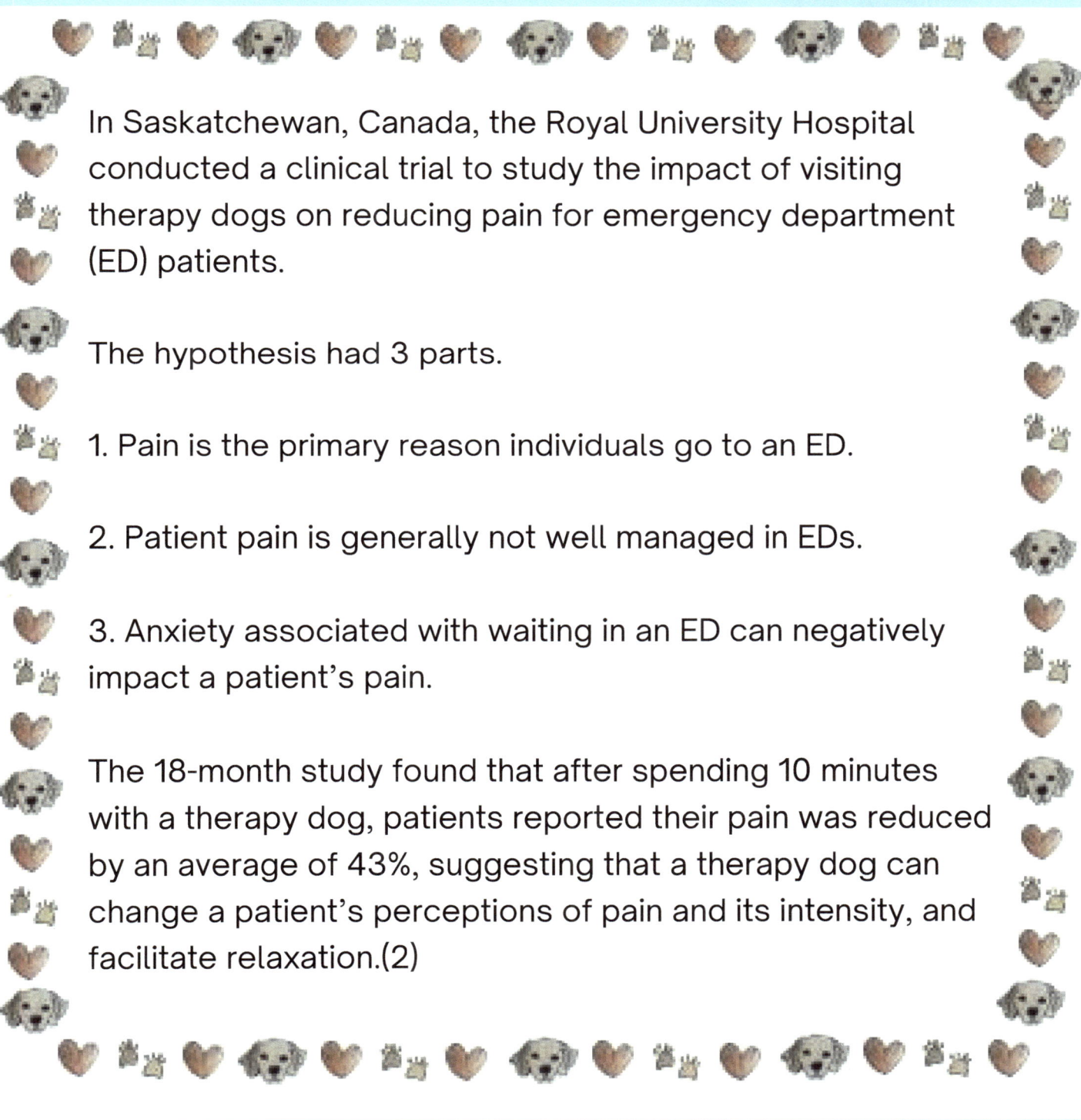

In Saskatchewan, Canada, the Royal University Hospital conducted a clinical trial to study the impact of visiting therapy dogs on reducing pain for emergency department (ED) patients.

The hypothesis had 3 parts.

1. Pain is the primary reason individuals go to an ED.

2. Patient pain is generally not well managed in EDs.

3. Anxiety associated with waiting in an ED can negatively impact a patient's pain.

The 18-month study found that after spending 10 minutes with a therapy dog, patients reported their pain was reduced by an average of 43%, suggesting that a therapy dog can change a patient's perceptions of pain and its intensity, and facilitate relaxation.(2)

Therapy dogs in nursing homes and hospitals bring comfort, support, laughter, and smiles to staff, residents, and patients – attachments form and relationships are built. Therapy dogs provide a welcome break from the routine, reduce anxiety and lower blood pressure.

The study at the Royal University Hospital also showed that 10 minutes with a therapy dog can decrease anxiety by 48%, decrease depression by 46%, and increase general well-being by 41%.(2)

Research at Johns Hopkins Medicine has shown that petting a dog lowers the stress hormone cortisol, while interaction between people and dogs increases levels of the feel-good hormone oxytocin.(3)

Pet vs. Assistance Dogs at a glance

	Pet Dogs	Therapy Dogs	Emotional Support Dogs	Service Dogs
Allowed in pet friendly facilities/locations	✔	✔	✔	✔
Registration/Certification from an organization required	✗	✔	✗	✗
Must wear identification when working	✗	✔	✗	✗
Permission required to enter non-pet friendly facilities/locations	✗	✔	✗	✗
Provides emotional support to <u>many</u> people	✗	✔	✗	✗
Provides emotional support to <u>one</u> person	✗	✗	✔	✗
May live anywhere, even if pets are not allowed	✗	✗	✔	✔
Requires a medical diagnosis	✗	✗	✔	✔
May enter non-pet friendly facilities/locations without permission	✗	✗	✗	✔
Trained to perform tasks for one person with a disability or medical condition*	✗	✗	✗	✔
Public access rights, including restaurants, stores, and airplanes**	✗	✗	✗	✔

*The Americans with Disabilities Act (ADA) allows facilities to ask only 2 questions of dog owners: 1) Is the dog a service animal required because of a disability? 2) What work or task has the dog been trained to perform? Note: Facilities cannot request proof.

**The Air Carriers Access Act (ACAA) does not grant Emotional Support Dogs (ESD) the right to access airplanes; however, some airlines do permit ESDs to travel in the cabin. If you plan to travel with an ESD, check with your airline before you book your flight.

Want to find out more about therapy dogs?

Check out these websites:

golden-dogs.org (Bright & Beautiful Therapy Dogs)

therapydogs.com

akc.org/products-services/training-programs/akc-therapy-dog-program/

Sources:

ada.gov

https://www.transportation.gov/individuals/aviation-consumer-protection/service-animals

(1) Smith, M. H., & Meehan, C. L. (2012). The impact of reading aloud to dogs on the reading skills of school-aged children: Results from two exploratory studies. Unpublished manuscript. Department of Population Health and Reproduction, School of Veterinary Medicine, University of California, Davis, California.
https://www.ucdavis.edu/news/reading-rover-does-it-really-help-children-veterinary-school-says-%E2%80%98yes%E2%80%99
https://ucanr.edu/delivers/?impact=800
hud.gov/program_offices/fair_housing_equal_opp/assistance_animals

(2) Pawsitive Impacts of Therapy Dog Visits, Sponsor: University of Saskatchewan, Collaborator: Royal University Hospital Foundation, Results Posted: November 5, 2021, Clinical Trial #: NCT04727749
https://clinicaltrials.gov/ct2/show/NCT04727749

(3) The Friend Who Keeps You Young, John Hopkins Medicine,
https://www.hopkinsmedicine.org/health/wellness-and-prevention/the-friend-who-keeps-you-young/

Want to find out more about therapy dogs?

Check out these websites:

golden-dogs.org (Bright & Beautiful Therapy Dogs)

therapydogs.com

akc.org/products-services/training-programs/akc-therapy-dog-program/

Sources:

ada.gov

https://www.transportation.gov/individuals/aviation-consumer-protection/service-animals

(1) Smith, M. H., & Meehan, C. L. (2012). The impact of reading aloud to dogs on the reading skills of school-aged children: Results from two exploratory studies. Unpublished manuscript. Department of Population Health and Reproduction, School of Veterinary Medicine, University of California, Davis, California.
https://www.ucdavis.edu/news/reading-rover-does-it-really-help-children-veterinary-school-says-%E2%80%98yes%E2%80%99
https://ucanr.edu/delivers/?impact=800
hud.gov/program_offices/fair_housing_equal_opp/assistance_animals

(2) Pawsitive Impacts of Therapy Dog Visits, Sponsor: University of Saskatchewan, Collaborator: Royal University Hospital Foundation, Results Posted: November 5, 2021, Clinical Trial #: NCT04727749
https://clinicaltrials.gov/ct2/show/NCT04727749

(3) The Friend Who Keeps You Young, John Hopkins Medicine,
https://www.hopkinsmedicine.org/health/wellness-and-prevention/the-friend-who-keeps-you-young/

About the author

Katie Baron lives in rural Sussex County, New Jersey, with her husband Joe, Archer the Therapy Dog, and Geordi, therapy dog in-training. Katie is a passionate advocate for the benefits of therapy dogs and increasing awareness about the public access rights of different types of working dogs.

About the illustrator

Emily Beach is a middle school student who lives in New Jersey with her parents, her sister, and her cat, Peter. Emily was the first child to read to Archer at the Read to a Dog program at the library. Emily loves all animals and when she grows up, she hopes to be a zoologist.

About Archer

Archer is a fun-loving Golden Retriever who loves swimming, playing keep away, and belly rubs. Archer started training to become a therapy dog when he was just 13 weeks old. After 2 years of training and hard work, he passed the test to become a Therapy Dog in October 2020, in the middle of the Covid 19 pandemic. He and Momma began weekly therapy dog visits at a local nursing home in August 2021, then started working with a local library as part of their Read to a Dog Program. Archer currently makes weekly visits at a nursing home and 2 schools. Archer's Instagram account (@archerthetherapydog) is dedicated to encouraging humans and dogs to be great therapy dog teams.